Text copyright © 1992 by Jon Blake
Illustrations copyright © 1992 by Axel Scheffler

First U.S. edition 1992
First published in Great Britain in 1992 by Walker Books Ltd., London.
ISBN 1-56402-078-9
Library of Congress Catalog Card Number 91-58725
Library of Congress Cataloging-in-Publication information is available.

10 9 8 7 6 5 4 3 2 1

Printed in Hong Kong

The illustrations in this book are watercolor,
crayon, and ink paintings.

Candlewick Press
2067 Massachusetts Avenue
Cambridge, Massachusetts 02140

Daley B.

by
Jon Blake

illustrated by
Axel Scheffler

CANDLEWICK PRESS
CAMBRIDGE, MASSACHUSETTS

Daley B. didn't
know what
he was.

"Am I a monkey?" he said.
"Am I a koala?"
"Am I a porcupine?"

Daley B. didn't know where to live.

"Should I live
in a cave?"
he said.

"Should I live in a nest?"

"Should I live in a web?"

Daley B. didn't know what to eat.

"Should I
eat fish?"
he said.

"Should I eat potatoes?"

"Should I eat worms?"

Daley B. didn't know why his feet were so big.

"Are they for water-skiing?" he said.

"Are they for the mice to sit on?"

"Are they to keep the rain off?"

Daley B. saw the birds in the tree and
decided he would live in a tree.

Daley B. saw the squirrels eating acorns
and decided he would eat acorns.

But he still didn't know why his feet were so big.

One day there was great panic in the
woods. All the rabbits gathered
beneath Daley B.'s tree.
"You must come down at
once, Daley B.!" they cried.
"Jazzy D. is coming!"
"Who is Jazzy D.?" asked Daley B.
The rabbits were too excited to answer.
They scattered across the grass and
vanished into their burrows.

Daley B. stayed in his tree, nibbled another acorn, and wondered about his big feet.

Jazzy D. crept out of the bushes.
Her teeth were as sharp as broken glass, and
her eyes were as quick as fleas.

Jazzy D. sneaked around the burrows, but
there was not a rabbit to be seen.

Jazzy D. looked up.
Daley B. waved.

Jazzy D. began to climb the tree.
The other rabbits poked out their
noses and trembled.

"Hello," said Daley B. to Jazzy D.

"Are you a badger?"

"Are you an elephant?"

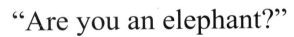

"Are you a duck-billed platypus?"

Jazzy D. crept closer. "No, my friend," she whispered. "I am a weasel."

"Do you live in a pond?" asked Daley B.

"Do you live in a dam?"

"Do you live in a kennel?"

Jazzy D. crept closer still.
"No, my friend," she hissed,
"I live in the darkest corner of the woods."

"Do you eat cabbages?" asked Daley B.

"Do you eat insects?"

"Do you eat fruit?"

Jazzy D. crept right up to Daley B.
"No, my friend," she rasped. "I eat rabbits!
Rabbits like *you*!"

Daley B.'s face fell.
"Am I … a rabbit?" he stammered.

Jazzy D. nodded . . . and licked her lips . . .

and *leapt!*

Daley B. didn't have to think. Quick as a
flash, he kicked out with his massive feet.
Jazzy D. sailed through the air, far far away,
back where she came from.

The other rabbits jumped and cheered
and hugged each other.
"You're a hero, Daley B.!" they cried.

"That's funny," said Daley B.
"I thought I was
a rabbit."